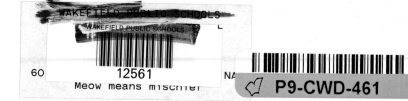

Meow Means Mischief

by
Ann Whitehead Nagda

illustrated by
Stephanie Roth

HOLIDAY HOUSE / NEW YORK

Library of Congress Cataloging-in-Publication Data

Nagda, Ann Whitehead, 1945–
Meow means mischief / by Ann Whitehead Nagda; illustrated by Stephanie Roth—1st ed.
p. cm.
Summary: A stray kitten turns out to be the perfect way
to help Rana make friends in her new school and to feel more comfortable
with her grandparents, who are visiting from India while her parents are away.
ISBN 0-8234-1786-7 (hardcover)
[1. Cats—Fiction. 2. Animals—Infancy—Fiction. 3. Grandparents—Fiction.
4. Schools—Fiction. 5. Moving, Household—Fiction. 6. East Indian Americans—
Fiction.] I. Roth, Stephanie, ill. II. Title.

PZ7.N13355 Me 2003
[Fic]—dc21
2002192208

For Asha
and Tigger
—A. W. N.

To Dweezel
—S. R.

She smiled. That was much better. Her two cousins were boys and they lived in India, close to her wrong grandma's apartment. She liked her other grandparents better. They lived in Pittsburgh.

My grandparents from India are going to stay with us for a whole week. They will take care of us while my parents go on a trip. We just moved into a new house. We haven't even unpacked all the boxes yet. We used to live in a different town. Our new house is bigger than our old house and has a big yard. I don't have to share a room with my sister now.

Rana chewed on her pencil. She needed to write some more. How do you describe a little sister?

My sister is five years old. Her name is Tara. She smells like bubble gum. Last year we went to India. My dad wanted us to see where he grew up. My grandma played with my sister. I am shy sometimes, especially with people I don't know very well. My sister is small and loud.

Chapter 1

The wrong grandma is coming to visit tonight. She never smiles at me. I don't think she likes me much. She likes my cousins more. My cousins are rough and fight a lot. I'm happy they live far away.

Rana stopped writing. She was supposed to be writing a journal entry, but she wasn't sure if she was doing it right. Everyone else in the class seemed to know what to do. But of course they would. They had been in the class since September. Rana had only been in the class since Monday.

Susan sat in front of her. She was bent over a thick spiral notebook. She wrote with a shiny ball-point pen.

Jenny sat beside Susan and wrote slowly with a pencil. Rana used a pencil, too—a yellow one that had tooth marks on it. Her tooth marks. Lots of them.

"Write what you feel in your journals," said Mrs. Steele, their teacher. "Describe things using all your senses—sounds and smells, too, not just what you see."

Mrs. Steele walked down the aisle and stopped by Rana. "That's a good start," she said softly. "Write some more about your cousins and your grandma."

Rana sighed and looked down at her paper. She picked up her pencil and twirled it between her fingers. Her new teacher was nice and she smelled good, too. She smelled like a rose.

My cousins smell like dirt.

Rana stopped and thought about smells and her cousins. Sometimes dirt smelled good, especially after a summer rain. She didn't want to say anything good about her cousins. She changed the sentence.

My cousins smell like dirty socks.

Richard, who sat next to Rana, threw down his pencil. It rolled off the desk and fell to the floor. He pushed his chair back, and it hit the desk behind him with a *thwack*. Richard was large and loud.

Susan turned and frowned at Richard. Then she looked at Rana and smiled. "You should use a notebook for your journal," she said.

"I don't have one yet," said Rana. She was using a single sheet of lined paper.

"I have an extra one," said Susan, reaching into her desk. "Here, you can have it. We're going to be keeping a journal all year long."

Rana hadn't made any friends in her new class yet. Maybe nobody liked her because she looked different. She bet no one else in the class had a mother with white skin and a father with brown skin. Eagerly Rana took the spiral notebook. Maybe Susan would be her friend.

"Put today's date on the top of the first page," said Susan. "Then write your entry for today in the notebook." Susan held up her journal for Rana to see. "Do it like this."

Rana looked at Susan's journal. She had written a whole page. Her handwriting was small and even and neat. Everything about Susan was neat. Her long blond hair was held in place with flowered barrettes. Her shirt had roses on it as well.

Rana opened the notebook to the first page. She picked up her pencil.

"I think pen looks nicer than pencil," said Susan. "Don't you have a pen?"

Rana shook her head. Were they supposed to use a pen?

Jenny turned around and rolled her eyes. "I use a pencil," said Jenny.

Susan tossed her head. "A pencil is fine if you make a lot of mistakes."

"It's your feelings that matter in a journal," said Jenny. "It's okay to make mistakes."

Susan turned around again and read what Rana had written in her journal. "I like your first sentence. It makes me want to read more."

Rana felt a small burst of pride. Susan liked her. A little bit, anyway.

"Hey, Susan," said Richard, "can I borrow your pen? My pencil doesn't work."

Susan frowned at Richard. "Use the pencil sharpener," she said.

Richard grabbed his pencil and got up. As he passed Susan's desk, he banged into it. Susan's notebook and pen went flying.

"You're so clumsy," Susan said.

"This is supposed to be writing time," said Mrs. Steele, "not talking time."

Rana bent over her new notebook. She wrote "November 5" at the top of the first page. Then she copied what she had written. She stared at the page. She needed to write more. Rana sighed.

It must have been a loud sigh, because Jenny turned around and looked at her. Then Jenny whispered, "You can write anything that comes into your head—trips you've taken or something that made you sad or angry or scared."

"Okay," said Rana. "Thanks."

Jenny smiled, then turned back to her journal.

Maybe Jenny would be her friend, too. Rana chewed on her pencil. What made her scared? Going to a new school where she didn't know anybody was scary. Not having any friends to talk to was scary. But she couldn't write about that. She didn't want anyone, especially her new teacher, to think she was a scaredy-cat.

She wrote:

My grandma and grandpa have an apartment in Bombay. That's a big city in India. They have a woman who cooks for them. She is short and fat. My dad told me many people in India don't get enough to eat. It's probably good to work as a cook there. My grandparents never eat meat. Their cook makes rice and vegetables for them to eat. They have another servant too. He serves water in tall glasses. The water has to be boiled. You can never drink water from the tap, because it will make you sick. I wish my parents weren't going away. I wish my grandparents weren't coming at all.

Chapter 2

When Rana got home from school, her mother was pushing the vacuum into the family room. That's where her grandparents were going to sleep. Cartons were stacked along one wall. The room was a mess.

"We've got two hours to clean this place," said Mom.

"Better get a magic wand," said Rana, looking around. "It's our only hope."

"I'll get my princess wand," said her little sister, Tara.

"Oh, great," Rana muttered. She watched her sister run down the hall, hair flying.

"Maybe they'd rather stay in a hotel," said Rana. "Or even a tent outside. Dad's pup tent."

Mom giggled. "I'm sure your grandma wouldn't like camping," she said.

The thought of Grandma crawling into a tent was silly. Rana had never seen her wear anything but a sari. A sari was a long dress, made from a big piece of material that Grandma wrapped around her body. It would get tangled if Grandma had to crawl into a tent.

Tara ran into the room waving her wand. It was pink with a big gold star at the end. Strips of shiny gold foil hung around the star. Tara started digging in one of the boxes with her wand. A ball of newspaper flew into the air.

"Rana, help her," her mother said. "There might be breakable dishes in that box."

The phone rang, and Mom went to answer it.

Rana was kneeling to unwrap some cups when she glanced toward the sliding-glass door. Standing there with its face pressed against the window was a little cat. Rana set the cup down and crawled over to the window. The kitty looked into her eyes,

then meowed. Rana slid the door open. The kitten pranced inside and meowed again. It had the tiniest, saddest meow.

"What's the matter, kitty?" said Rana. The cat was small, with black and gray stripes and tiny white feet. Its fur was matted and scruffy.

"Where did the kitty come from?" asked Tara. Still holding her wand, she walked over to the cat. The cat jumped up and swiped the wand with its paw. Tara held the wand higher. The cat leaped again and again.

"Wow! Look at the kitty jump!" said Rana.

"It will break my wand!" cried Tara. She held the wand behind her. The cat followed the wand.

"The kitty is just being playful," said Rana. "It won't hurt your wand."

Tara put the wand on the floor and sat down. The cat sniffed the wand. "No!" said Tara, pushing the cat away.

The cat swatted her. What a stubborn little thing, Rana thought. And clever, too.

"That bad kitty hurt me," Tara wailed, holding her arm.

"Let me see," said Rana, kneeling by her sister. "It's a tiny scratch. I'll kiss it and make it better."

The kitten rubbed against Rana's leg. She stroked its furry head. "Are you hungry, kitty?" she asked. She picked the cat up. It put both paws on her shoulder. Rana hugged the kitty tight. "You're a smart kitty, aren't you? You know I'll take care of you." She carried it into the kitchen and opened the refrigerator. "How about some milk, kitty?" she said. Rana set the kitten on the counter and lifted the big bottle out of the refrigerator.

Tara came into the kitchen. She was still holding her wand. "I wish I could wave my wand and turn the cat into a little bunny. I'd like to have a bunny for a pet."

Rana scowled at her sister as she got a bowl from the cupboard. Bunnies were cute, but cats were more fun to play with. She poured milk into the bowl. Some spilled on the counter and dripped onto the floor. The cat leaned over the bowl and lapped the milk with its tongue.

Her mother's footsteps echoed in the hallway.

"What in the world are you doing?" she said. "What is that cat doing on my nice clean countertop?"

"The kitty's hungry, Mom," said Rana. "It was on the porch looking in the window like it belonged here."

"Put the cat outside right now," said Mom.

"But it's starving," said Rana. "Look at it."

"You can put the bowl of milk outside, too," said Mom, softening her tone.

"I'll carry the bowl," said Tara, setting her wand on the counter. She tipped the bowl as she picked it up and spilled milk onto her shoes and the floor.

"I'll carry the bowl," said Mom firmly.

Rana carried the cat outside. It meowed over and over.

"Come inside now and help me," said Mom.

"I wish we could keep the kitty," said Rana.

"Well, we can't," said Mom. "The cat probably has a home."

"I don't think so," said Rana. With one final pat, she stood up. "Bye, kitty," she said softly.

Chapter 3

It was evening by the time Dad brought Grandma and Grandpa home from the airport. Grandma came gliding into the living room. "I like the new house," she said as she thrust her coat at Mom, then straightened her purple silk sari.

Dad and Grandpa staggered inside. They both carried heavy bags. They were the royal coachmen. Grandma was her royal highness, the queen.

Tara ran down the hall, waving her wand. "Grandma!" she cried. "Come see my new room." She threw her arms around Grandma's legs. Grandma leaned over and kissed her. "How's my sweet girl!" she said.

Tara was the little princess. Rana felt like she and her mother were the royal servants.

"Show me the downstairs first," said Grandma.

Tara grabbed Grandma's hand, pulling her past the dining room. "We can eat here sometimes," said Tara, "or in the kitchen."

"Very nice," said Grandma. "And who sleeps here?" She pointed to the family room.

"That's where you and Grandpa will sleep," said Rana, "on the couch."

Grandma shook her head. "This won't do at all. It's part of the kitchen and there's no privacy . . ." She looked like she was in pain. "And it's so messy."

"I tried to fix the room with my magic wand," said Tara, "but it didn't work."

"No, it obviously didn't," said Grandma, patting her head. She looked at Dad. "My dear, there must be a better place for us to sleep."

Grandpa set down the bags he was carrying. "This room is fine," he said.

"No, it isn't," snapped Grandma.

Dad looked at Mom. "How about Rana's room? We could move the cot in there."

Mom sighed. "Let's give them the master bedroom. We can sleep on the foldout couch tonight."

"Yes, that will do," said Grandma.

Of course that would do, thought Rana. You couldn't put royalty on a foldout couch.

Dad picked up the suitcases and carried them toward the stairs. Grandpa followed him.

Grandma sat down heavily in a kitchen chair. "It's such a long trip from India."

"Would you like something to drink?" said Mom. "Tea? Juice? Did you eat dinner on the plane?"

"They had very good service on the flight," said Grandma. "Now I would like some tea. And a small piece of cake."

"We don't have any cake," said Mom. "How about some cereal or an English muffin with jam?"

Grandma wrinkled her nose. "I don't feel like breakfast. Don't you cook anymore?"

Mom stared at Grandma.

"I can fix you some cinnamon toast," said Rana quickly.

"Cinnamon toast is good," said Tara. "You'll like it," she told Grandma. "I'll have some too."

Grandma smiled at Tara. "That sounds fine."

Rana fixed toast for Grandma and Tara. When she served it, only Tara said thank you.

Meanwhile Tara was talking all about the move

and the boxes and her new bedroom. With Tara around, no one else got to talk.

"Did you bring me a present?" asked Tara.

"We did," said Grandma, "but you'll have to wait until tomorrow. I'm too tired to unpack tonight."

"I can't wait!" Tara said happily.

Rana could wait. Her present was probably some weird clothing from India, like she got last year for Christmas. She didn't like to wear anything unusual. She felt different enough as it was.

After Grandma had her tea and toast, she followed Tara to see the new bedroom. Rana cleaned up. She noticed that Grandma left her toast crusts just like Tara did. No wonder they got along so well.

Rana wondered if the kitten was still on the porch. Where would a kitty spend the night if it had no place to live? She lifted the curtain and peered out. She didn't see the kitty. She wished the little cat would come back and Grandma would go away.

Chapter 4

This morning a small gray cat was on our porch again. It looked in the window. I sneaked outside and gave the kitty half of my scrambled eggs. The kitty ate them very fast. The kitty was there yesterday too. I hope the kitty will stay and be my pet. I only wish I knew how to take care of a cat.

Mrs. Steele put her hand on Rana's shoulder and leaned over to read her journal entry. "I like that a lot," she said. "Write more about the kitten. Is it fat or thin? What color are its eyes?"

Mrs. Steele stopped by Richard's desk. "Are you having trouble with your writing today?" she asked him.

"I can't think of anything to write about," he said.

"You could write about something you did after school yesterday," Mrs. Steele suggested. "Or about your brother? Or a best friend?"

"I could write about my brother, I guess," said Richard. "I could tell about letting all the air out of the tires on his bicycle, so he couldn't follow me to the park."

"I could write a whole book on mean things I do to my sister," said Kevin.

Rana turned around to look at Kevin. He wore a green shirt with a big lizard on it. She felt sorry for his sister.

"I think you should write about nice things as well," said Mrs. Steele.

"I'd have to do something nice first," said Kevin.

"Shhh. Try to work quietly," said Mrs. Steele.

She stopped by Susan's desk. Then she walked back to Rana. "Susan has a cat," she said quietly. "Maybe she could help you with the kitty."

"Would you ask her for me?" whispered Rana.

"Sure," Mrs. Steele whispered back. "I'll ask Susan to talk with you during recess."

When the recess bell rang, Susan turned to Rana. "Mrs. Steele said you needed some help with your kitty," she said.

"It's not my kitty yet," said Rana, "but I've been feeding it." She and Susan walked outside and sat on the swings.

"I think cats are the best pets," said Susan. "My cat sits in my lap when I read a book."

"This kitty is striped like a tiger," said Rana. "I think it looks lonely."

"I can come to your house after school," said Susan. "I'm sure it will be okay with my mom."

"I'd like that," said Rana. But she wasn't sure if she wanted Susan to meet her grandparents.

When Rana and Susan got home from school, only Grandpa was there. He was sitting in the family room reading the paper. Grandma had gone food shopping with Rana's mother and sister. Rana hoped they shopped a long time.

"This is Susan, Grandpa," said Rana. "She's going to help me with the kitty. If it's still here."

Grandpa put down his paper. "I saw the cat on the porch a little while ago." He smiled at Susan. "I'm happy to meet one of Rana's friends," he said.

Rana rushed to the window. The kitten was

sleeping on the porch railing. Rana opened the door and went outside.

Susan followed her and picked up the cat, holding it like a baby. The kitten opened its eyes and yawned.

"I think it's a female," said Susan, "just like my cat."

"She is so sweet," said Rana, patting the cat's head.

"The kitten's fur is muddy," said Susan. "I don't think she has a home. So you can keep her."

"I don't think my mom will let me," said Rana.

"She has to!" said Susan. "Do you have any cat food or a litter box?"

Rana shook her head. "We never had a cat before."

"I'll call my mom and ask her to bring some things over when she comes to pick me up," said Susan, carrying the cat inside. She handed the cat to Rana, then called her mom. After she used the phone, she said, "We should give the kitty a bath. Once she looks better, your mom won't mind having her around."

Rana wasn't sure about that. Her mom had been very busy with working, the new house, and now

Grandma and Grandpa. She wouldn't be happy about a new pet. Even if it was adorable and had clean fur.

Susan walked over to the kitchen sink. "Good, you have one of those spray nozzles and a double sink. Now get two towels and we'll wash the kitty right here."

Rana handed her the kitten and ran upstairs to get the towels. When she returned, Susan was talking softly to the cat and rubbing her under the chin.

"I brought my sister's baby shampoo," said Rana.

"Good," said Susan. "Put one towel in the sink, so the cat can stand on it. Put the other towel on the counter to dry her off."

After Rana spread the towel in the sink, Susan placed the kitten on the towel. "You'll have to hold on to her," Susan said, "because cats hate water."

Susan moved the faucet to the other sink and turned on the water.

The cat leaped onto the counter. Susan grabbed her. "Maybe I'd better hold her," Susan said, putting the cat back in the sink and placing both hands around the cat's body behind the front legs. "Make sure the water is warm and then spray her."

Rana took the sprayer. She held her hand in the stream of water until it seemed warm enough. Still, she felt bad when she sprayed water on the cat's fur. The kitten tried to escape again, but Susan held her tight.

"Try not to get water on her head or in her eyes," said Susan.

Rana gently rubbed shampoo into the fur on the kitty's back. The cat tried to bite the sprayer. She squirmed while Rana washed the shampoo off. Rana hoped Susan really knew what she was doing, because the cat seemed scared and unhappy. She hoped the kitten wouldn't hate her for getting her wet and soapy.

"That's enough," said Susan, picking up the wet cat and placing her on the other towel. "Now wrap the towel around her and dry her off."

Rana dropped the sprayer and dabbed at the cat's fur with the towel. She didn't look like a cat anymore—she looked like a wet bird. Her fur was all clumped together, and she hunched down on the towel. Rana wrapped the end of the towel around the kitten's body and rubbed gently.

The cat broke loose, jumped to the floor, raced to the hallway, and rubbed one side of her face on the carpet. She turned her head and rubbed the other side of her face.

Susan took the towel and ran after the cat. The cat saw her coming and ran under the dining-room table.

Susan moved a chair and crawled under the table. The cat ran into the living room and hid under the coffee table.

"She'll be almost dry by the time we catch her," said Susan. She ran to one side of the coffee table while Rana went to the other side. The cat ran under Grandpa's legs.

"The cat runs very fast," said Grandpa.

Rana grabbed the cat before she could find another hiding place.

The doorbell rang. "I bet that's my mother," said Susan, hurrying to open the front door. Rana followed with the kitten.

"Mother, this is Rana," said Susan, "and this is her new kitty."

Susan's mother looked a lot like Susan. She had the same blond hair that curled at the ends and the same blue eyes. Rana wished she looked more like her own mother, but she didn't look like her at all. She looked more like her dad and her wrong grandma.

"It's nice to meet you, Rana," said Susan's mother. She handed a large grocery bag to Susan. "Let me hold that sweet little kitten," she said. As Rana held the cat out, Susan's mother said, "She must be about six or seven months old." She took the kitten and held her close to her face. "Oh, you are just precious."

Susan looked inside the bag. "Some cat food, some litter, and our spare litter box. I still have a few more things to show Rana," she told her mother, "so I'll walk home."

"Come home before dark." Susan's mother handed the kitten to Rana and said, "Good luck with your new kitty."

"Thank you so much," said Rana. Susan and her mother were being so kind. Rana felt like it was her birthday.

Chapter 5

Rana carried the kitten to the kitchen. Susan carried the bag of supplies.

"Are you hungry, kitty?" Rana stood on a chair to get a bowl and a plate from the cabinet. As she handed them to Susan, she noticed the mess they'd made. The towel in the sink was wet and had mud on it. There were puddles on the counter. Water had dripped onto the floor. It looked like a giant monster had taken a bath, not a small kitty. She'd have to hurry and get everything cleaned up before her mother got home.

Susan opened a small can of "Seafood Delight" and put some on the plate. She set the plate on the floor, then sat down beside it.

The cat sniffed the food and started eating immediately.

Rana leaned down so she could watch the kitty eat. The cat's pink tongue was moving very fast, licking the food, then scooping some up, then licking some more. Either the kitty was very hungry, or the food tasted better than it looked.

Hearing footsteps in the hall, Rana jerked upright.

"Oh, no," said Rana's mother, walking into the kitchen. "What happened here?"

Uh-oh. Her mom was mad. Rana felt her face get hot. "I—I washed the kitty," Rana explained, "and now I'm feeding her. Susan came home with me today. She's in my class at school. She showed me how to take care of the kitty."

"That was very nice of Susan, but . . ." Rana's mother wrinkled her forehead and rubbed one side of her head with two fingers. It was a headache kind of rub. "Honey, I don't have time to take care of a pet."

"I can take care of the kitty," said Rana. "I can do everything. I'll clean up the kitchen right away, too."

"I just don't want the responsibility of an animal right now," said her mother firmly.

Rana jumped up and started mopping the water on the counter. Maybe her mother would change her mind when the kitchen was spotless. Susan helped her.

Tara entered the kitchen, followed by Grandma.

"That's the bad kitty that scratched me," Tara said, pointing to the kitten.

"I don't like cats," said Grandma. She set a bag of groceries by the refrigerator.

Grandpa walked over. He picked up the kitten. "In India people always feed stray animals, even poor people."

"Why do they do that, Grandpa, even when they're poor?" asked Rana.

Grandpa smiled at her. "You never know in what form God will come to your door."

"You mean the kitty might be a god?" asked Rana.

"We believe that God comes in many disguises." He looked at Rana's mother. "It wouldn't be right to put this poor animal back out in the cold."

Mom sighed. "The kitty can stay until your father and I get back from our trip," she said, "and then we'll decide."

Rana smiled at Grandpa. She was really glad he'd come to visit. Maybe next time he'd leave Grandma at home.

Chapter 6

After giving Rana some more tips on cat care, Susan left. Rana finished cleaning up the kitchen, then took the cat into the family room. She sat on the couch with Grandpa while he watched the news. The kitten snuggled down on Rana's legs. Rana ran her fingers between the kitten's ears and along her back. The kitten started to purr. It sounded like a little motor was running.

"Susan told me that when a cat purrs, it means 'I'm happy and I like you,'" Rana told Grandpa.

"Maybe the kitty's forgotten about her bath this afternoon."

Grandpa patted the cat's back. "Have you given her a name yet?"

"She looks like a little tiger," said Rana.

"Come here, Tiger," said Grandpa. The kitten opened her eyes and looked at Grandpa, but she didn't move from Rana's lap.

"Do you like the name Tiger?" asked Rana. She stroked the kitten's head and the kitten purred louder.

"That sounds like a yes to me," said Grandpa.

Rana held the cat up to her face. "Now, Tiger," she said, "you have to be very good, so that Mom will let me keep you."

Tiger struggled to get down. Rana let her go, and she bounded toward the window. After peering outside, Tiger leaped onto Rana's lap again. The kitty was like a small fur blanket. Where the cat lay, Rana's legs were toasty and warm.

Her mother leaned over the sofa and said, "Honey, I need help with the laundry."

Rana put Tiger on the sofa and carried some clean clothes upstairs for her mother. When she came back downstairs, Tiger was gone.

Then she heard Grandma say, "That cat is trying to eat our dinner."

Rana rushed into the kitchen. Sure enough, Tiger was perched on the counter. Grandma had made the dough for chapatis, Indian bread. Tiger stretched out a paw and snagged a bit of dough on her claws.

"No, no," said Grandma, waving her rolling pin at the cat.

The cat batted the rolling pin with her paw.

"No, Tiger!" Rana picked up the kitten and set her on the floor. Tiger looked up at the counter and leaped onto it. Rana put her down again. Tiger leaped back onto the counter. The kitten was like a yo-yo. Rana giggled.

Grandma turned her head and gave the cat a stern look. "That cat is trouble," she said.

Rana put the cat on the floor one more time, but Tiger immediately jumped back onto the counter. Maybe she should have named the kitty Trouble. Tiger sniffed the glasses by the sink.

Rana watched as Grandma rolled a piece of dough into a perfect circle. When she checked on Tiger, Rana saw her lick a stick of butter. It was the butter Grandma was going to rub on the cooked chapatis. Rana pulled Tiger away and held her. There were tiny curved scratches on the butter. Rana hoped Grandma wouldn't notice. Or her

mom. She carried the naughty kitten to her room. She sat on her bed and showed Tiger her stuffed animals. Tiger sniffed them one by one, then she lay down next to the big teddy bear. Rana liked to cuddle with that bear, too.

"Rana, please come and set the table," her mother called.

Rana shut the door as she left her room.

Grandma had made the entire dinner. Her mother had been busy packing for their trip. They were leaving right after dinner.

Rana took a bite of potato and pea mixture. It burned her tongue and made her eyes water. She gulped down half a glass of milk. Her tongue still burned. She ate some chapati and then some yogurt. Her tongue felt better. She hated it when Grandma cooked. The food was always too spicy.

"Great food, Mummy," said her father. "These are the best potatoes."

Rana stared at him in surprise. His mouth must be fireproof.

Tara, meanwhile, was eating and eating. Her eyes weren't watering at all.

After dinner, Grandma brought out presents. She gave both Rana and Tara matching skirts and blouses from India. The material was beautiful with sparkly metal circles sewed onto it, but Rana knew she'd never wear it.

"This is pretty, Grandma," said Tara.

Grandma smiled. She gave Mom a fancy belt and Dad a silk shirt with flowers on it. Rana had never seen her father wear a flowered shirt.

Grandma opened a big bag at her feet. She pulled out what looked like a doll with fancy clothes and a wooden head. Black strings connected the head and hands to a wooden bar. "When we were in Rajasthan last month, we bought puppets," Grandma said. "This one is for Rana."

"Thank you!" said Rana, taking the puppet from Grandma. The puppet was beautiful. She ran her fingers across the doll's fancy skirt. It was the best present her grandparents had ever given her.

"Rajasthan is in northern India," Grandpa said. "That's where I was born."

"I have a puppet for Tara, too," said Grandma. She held out another puppet.

Tara took the wooden bar. The strings were connected to a man riding a horse. "Wow!" she said. "But why doesn't my horse have legs?"

"Most of the puppets from northern India have

skirts instead of legs," said Grandma. "The royal families wore long skirts like this hundreds of years ago."

"Even the men?" asked Rana.

"Even the men," said Grandma.

"But what about horses?" said Tara.

"The horses wore skirts when they went into battle," said Grandpa.

"I love the puppets!" said Rana. She smiled at Grandma, and Grandma smiled at her.

Dad looked at his watch. "We have to leave for the airport now," he said.

"The phone number for our hotel is on the refrigerator," Mom told Grandma and Grandpa. She hugged Rana. "Remember to help your grandparents," she said.

Rana went to her room. Her parents wouldn't be back until Wednesday. That was a long time. She whispered into Tiger's fur. "Can you stay out of trouble for seven days?"

The kitten said, *"Meow."* It sounded like "Nooooo way."

Chapter 7

My grandmother gave me a beautiful puppet from India. But the best present of all is my kitten. Susan helped me give her a bath. I named her Tiger, because she has stripes. Mom said we could keep the kitten until she gets back from her trip. I hope we'll keep the kitten forever. I'm glad Mom didn't see Tiger lick the butter.

Susan leaned over and said, "How's the cat?"

"Great!" said Rana. "She slept by my feet all night long."

"Did she wake you up early?" asked Susan.

"Yes," said Rana. "She stood on my pillow right next to my head and purred. When I wouldn't open my eyes, she licked my eyelids."

"Somebody slimed your eyelids?" said Richard.

Rana turned to him, laughing. "My new cat licked them. Her tongue felt like sandpaper—all rough and scratchy."

"There's too much talking," said Mrs. Steele, "and not enough writing."

"Oops." Susan leaned over her notebook.

Rana thought about the scratches in the butter. Maybe she had scratches on her eyelids. She closed her eyes and ran her fingertip along one eyelid. It felt smooth and soft. So did the other eyelid. She smiled when she thought about the wild kitty. Her grandma didn't like Tiger. She wished her other grandma had come to stay with them instead. Her other grandma would love the small kitten. Her other grandma made food that Rana liked, not spicy food that burned her tongue.

Grandma made dinner last night. She made potatoes that burned my mouth and made my eyes water. I wish I could eat cat food for the next seven days.

Mrs. Steele stood in front of the room. "Would anyone like to read a journal entry to the class?"

Rana thought their journal entries were supposed to be private. She closed her notebook. She certainly didn't want to have to read what she'd written to the whole class.

Kevin raised his hand.

"Yes, Kevin," said Mrs. Steele. "Come stand next to me."

Kevin stomped to the front of the room. He read, "My little sister is a pain. She follows me around when I get home from school. Sometimes she takes my toys. I took her favorite baby doll and hid it in my closet."

Some of the kids laughed. Mrs. Steele didn't. She said, "It sounds like your sister likes you a lot, Kevin."

Kevin shrugged and went back to his seat.

"Anyone else?" said Mrs. Steele.

Susan raised her hand. She walked to the front of the room with a big smile on her face and read from her notebook. "Yesterday I went to Rana's house. I showed her how to take care of her new kitten. We gave the kitten a bath. We also gave her some food and set up the litter box. Rana's grandparents are visiting. They live in India and their skin is dark, darker than Rana's."

Rana felt her face get hot. She wished Susan would stop. She didn't want anyone to know about her grandmother and grandfather. When Susan wrote about Rana's skin color, it made her feel even more different.

But Susan read on and on. "Rana's grandmother wears pretty, long dresses. The dress she had on yesterday had a green background with white designs on it. Her grandfather wore ordinary men's clothing. Only her grandmother wore traditional Indian clothing."

"How nice of you to help Rana with her kitten," said Mrs. Steele. "And that is interesting about their clothing. Would you like to add anything, Rana?"

Rana felt her face get even hotter. No, she didn't want to say anything. The classroom was deadly still. Everyone was looking at her. She swallowed. "My grandfather works in a bank." She looked around the room. Everyone was still staring at her. "He always wears suits." She looked down at her desk. She could see Susan's feet coming up the aisle, but Rana didn't look up.

At recess, Rana left quickly and joined Richard

and Jenny outside. She tried to avoid Susan, but Susan found her right away.

"What's wrong, Rana? Are you mad at me?" asked Susan.

Rana looked down and kicked a stone with her shoe.

Susan took Rana's arm and pulled her away from Richard and Jenny. "Are you mad because I read my journal entry about your family?" she asked.

"Yes," said Rana. "I didn't want anyone to talk about my grandparents. They're so different." Her voice shook and she could feel her lower lip quiver.

"I'm sorry, Rana," said Susan. "I think your grandparents are neat."

"You do?" said Rana.

"I loved what your grandpa said about feeding stray animals," said Susan. "And your grandmother was wearing a beautiful dress."

"I don't like being different," said Rana.

"You're lucky," said Susan. "I wish I had grandparents like yours. I only have one grandma left, and she's in a nursing home. She doesn't even know who I am."

"That's sad," said Rana.

"Please don't be mad at me anymore," said Susan.

"It's not okay to say things about my family without asking me first," said Rana.

"I'm sorry," said Susan.

After recess, Rana finished her math problems quickly. Then she wrote in her journal.

I'm mad at Susan, because she told the class about my grandparents. She said their skin was darker than mine. I wanted to crawl under my desk and hide. I thought Susan was my friend. She said she was sorry at recess. But I'm still mad.

Chapter 8

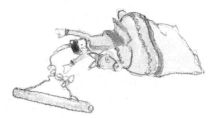

When Rana got home from school, she looked for Tiger right away. She found her asleep in Grandpa's lap.

"How's Tiger been today, Grandpa?" she asked.

"The cat wanted to read the newspaper with me this morning," said Grandpa. "So she sat on the paper." Grandpa rubbed the kitty's back. "Maybe it's a good thing she sleeps a lot."

Tiger opened her eyes lazily, then shut them again. Her tail flicked back and forth slowly.

Rana picked up the kitty. "Come here, lazy bones," she said. The cat was warm and cuddly. Rana kissed the top of her head.

Tara danced into the family room, carrying her puppet and Rana's as well. "Let's have a puppet show," she said, holding out Rana's puppet.

Rana looked at her puppet. "The strings are all tangled," she said.

"Maybe the cat did it," said Tara.

Tiger grabbed a string with her paw and chewed on it.

"Tiger, you're not helping," said Rana. She put the cat down and untangled the puppet's strings.

"My puppet will ride into town on his horse," said Tara. She moved her puppet near her sister's. "Help, help, somebody stole all my money."

"Oh, no," said Rana, moving her puppet's arms up and down. "Who did it?"

"I was asleep," said Tara. "I don't know who did it."

"Where were you sleeping?" said Rana, moving her puppet again.

The kitten stood up. She watched the puppets.

"Under my horse," said Tara.

"Why were you sleeping under your horse?" said Rana.

"It was raining," said Tara.

The kitten crept to the edge of the couch. Her ears swiveled forward.

"And your horse kept you dry?" said Rana.

"Yes. The horse has a skirt," said Tara. "It's like sleeping in a tent."

Rana laughed, and so did Grandpa.

"Well, it does," said Tara. She made her horse gallop back and forth.

Tiger jumped to the ground and leaped at Tara's puppet.

"No, no! Bad cat!" screamed Tara.

Grandma came into the family room.

"We're having a puppet show," said Grandpa.

Rana made her puppet dance. The kitty leaped at her puppet. Rana pulled it away. The kitty leaped

again. Then Tiger leaped at Tara's horse. The kitten stood on her back legs and pawed at the strings. Suddenly one of the strings snapped.

"That bad cat broke my puppet!" Tara wailed. Tears rolled down her cheeks.

Grandma pursed her lips. "Oh, dear," she said, taking the puppet.

Tara climbed into Grandma's lap, sobbing.

Grandma hugged Tara. "I can fix the puppet." Grandma tied a knot in the string. "Now put the cat outside," she said in a stern voice.

Rana picked up the kitten, opened the door, and set her down. She watched as Tiger bounded off the porch and disappeared into the bushes. She hoped her kitten knew where her home was. This was the first time they'd let her go outside. What if she found a new family? Rana walked slowly back to the family room.

Grandma stood up. "Now it's time to prepare dinner," she said. "Rana, come and help me."

Rana followed Grandma to the kitchen.

"You chop the vegetables while I make the chapatis," said Grandma. She put a bowl of fresh green beans and two onions next to the cutting board.

Oh, no, not onions, Rana thought. She picked up a green bean and cut it into four pieces. "Make the pieces smaller," said Grandma, "like this." She cut one bean into a dozen pieces.

It took forever to cut up the beans. Rana put all the bean pieces in the bowl and stared at the two onions. "Grandma, onions make me cry," she said.

"That's just the way onions are," said Grandma. "Here, let me show you how to get the skin off." Grandma took an onion and cut it in half. She removed the skin from both halves. "There, now you can cut it."

Rana took the knife. She made one slice, then another. Her eyes started to water.

"That's right," said Grandma. "Now make the pieces smaller."

Rana cut and cut. Her eyes watered more and more. She wiped her face on her sleeve.

"Good," said Grandma when Rana had finished cutting one onion. "Now watch while I cook the green-bean curry." Grandma heated oil in a skillet. She opened a round, silver container that she'd brought from India. It contained spices. Grandma filled a spoon with tiny black seeds and dropped them in the oil. Rana could hear them popping. "That's mustard seed," Grandma said. Next she added a spoonful of orange spice to the skillet. "Turmeric," she said. "Now for the cumin and coriander." She added several spoonfuls of brownish stuff to the skillet. She dipped her spoon into some red powder.

"Is that the stuff that burns my tongue?" asked Rana.

"This is red pepper," said Grandma. "Was the food too hot for you yesterday?"

"Yes," said Rana.

"Most Indian children your age can eat hot food," said Grandma. "I don't think Tara has a problem."

Grandma's words stung, but Rana noticed that she only shook a little red powder into the skillet. "And now we'll fry the onions." Grandma pushed the onions from the cutting board into the skillet. The onions sizzled.

"Cut the next onion for the potato curry," said Grandma.

Rana cut the onion in half. Her eyes started to water again. She felt something bump her leg. It was a kitty bump. "Tiger's back," she said. "How did she get in the house?"

Grandma screamed.

Rana wiped her eyes on her sleeve. The kitten had brought a small green and yellow snake into the kitchen. Tiger pushed at the snake with her paw. The snake moved. Tiger picked up the snake in her mouth and shook it. Rana backed away.

Grandpa came into the kitchen. "What's wrong?" he said calmly. He watched as the kitten pushed the snake again. The snake wriggled.

"Do something, Grandpa," said Rana.

"It's just a small snake," said Grandpa. He picked it up. "I'll put it outside."

Rana followed him through the family room. The cat followed Rana. Rana picked up the cat while Grandpa went outside with the snake.

Grandpa came back in and closed the sliding-glass door. "I put the snake in some bushes," he said.

"You're brave, Grandpa," said Rana.

"I grew up in a village," he told Rana. "There were lots of snakes around."

"Lots of poisonous snakes," said Grandma, her voice still shaking.

"Snakes are scary," said Tara.

"How did the cat get inside with the snake?" asked Grandma.

"She must have had it when I let her in," said Grandpa. "I was watching the news on TV, so I didn't pay much attention."

Suddenly there was a loud buzzing sound.

"It's the smoke alarm," said Rana.

Grandpa ran into the kitchen. Rana followed him. The skillet was smoking.

Grandpa took the skillet off the burner. He opened a window. Cold air blew into the kitchen. Still the alarm continued. He opened more windows. The buzzing finally stopped.

Grandma looked in the skillet. The onions were black. "You'll have to cut more onions, Rana," said Grandma.

Rana groaned. "First I'll put the kitten in my room," she said. She carried Tiger upstairs. She kissed the cat on the top of her head, then set her on the bed. "You mustn't scare Grandma like that," she said. "I won't be able to keep you if you bring any more snakes in the house."

Tiger sat on the bed and stared at Rana with her big green eyes.

By the time they ate dinner, it was late. Rana was very tired. As soon as she had eaten, she said good night to her grandparents and went up to her bedroom. When she opened the door, her room was dark except for two glowing marbles on her bed. They looked like monster eyes. She flipped on the light. Tiger sat on the bed. Her big green eyes stared at Rana. Rana turned off the light again. The cat's eyes glowed again like tiny flashlights in the dark.

After Rana put on her pajamas and got into bed, Tiger curled up next to her pillow. Rana had just turned off her light and closed her eyes when she heard a slurping sound. She turned on her light. Tiger was licking her paw. Over and over she licked one side of her paw. Then she rubbed it on the side of her face. Lick and rub, lick and rub. Soon she started to clean her chest. Slurp and lick, slurp and lick.

Rana put her head down on her pillow and watched the kitten give herself a spit bath. She touched the fur on the cat's chest. It was damp. Tiger licked Rana's finger over and over with her sandpaper tongue. Rana loved it. The cat was giving her a bath, too. When the kitten stopped spitting and licking, Rana fell asleep.

Chapter 9

When Rana woke up the next morning, she heard a funny sound, like a cough. She looked at the floor and saw that her kitten was throwing up. The small animal staggered a little, then threw up again.

Rana sprang out of bed. She stepped in something gooey. Yuck! It was kitty barf. "What's the matter?" said Rana, kneeling down and putting both hands on the cat. "Are you sick, little one?"

Tiger rubbed against her leg.

Rana looked around. There were three piles of yucky brown stuff on her rug. She looked closely at the one she had stepped in. There were hairs in it.

She picked the kitten up. Watching her feet, she tiptoed around the places where her cat had been

sick. She needed help. She rushed down the hall
calling for Grandpa.

Grandma came out of the master bedroom.

"Where's Grandpa?" asked Rana.

"He's taking his bath," said Grandma. "What's
wrong?"

"Something is wrong with Tiger. She threw up
in my room." Rana held Tiger out, but Grandma
ignored the cat and headed down the hall to Rana's
room. Rana followed her.

Grandma stood in the doorway and looked
around the room. She put her hand to her mouth, and

turned her head away. "You'll have to clean this up."

"I'm worried about Tiger," said Rana.

Tiger struggled, twisting and turning her small body until Rana put her on the floor. She meowed.

Rana knelt down. "What is it, Tiger?"

The kitten rubbed against her ankle again, then rubbed her head on Rana's hand.

"I think I should stay home with her," said Rana.

"You need to go to school," said Grandma, firmly. "But first you must clean your rug."

"I don't know how," said Rana.

"Now I have to help Tara get ready for kindergarten. The cat is your responsibility," said Grandma as she left the room.

Rana picked up the cat. She thought of Susan. She was still mad at her, but she needed help. The cat sat in her lap while she looked up Susan's number. She dialed with a trembling finger. She was glad to hear Susan's voice. "This is Rana. I'm worried about my cat." Rana took a deep breath. "She threw up."

"Was there hair in it?" asked Susan.

"Yes," said Rana.

"Then it's probably just a hair ball," said Susan. "Nothing to worry about."

"Really?" said Rana. "I was so scared." She

hugged the cat. "But how can I clean the rug?"

"My mother uses a spoon to scrape up the thick stuff," said Susan matter-of-factly.

Rana grimaced.

"Then she pours water and rug cleaner on the spot that's left," Susan went on, "then she presses a towel on the spot to get up the liquid."

Rana wished Susan's mother were at her house. "Okay, thanks," she told Susan.

Rana cleaned up the carpet as best she could. She hoped her mother wouldn't be able to see any spots later.

When Rana got to school, she went right to her classroom. It was early and no one was there. She found her journal in a stack on the teacher's desk. She looked inside to see if Mrs. Steele had made any comments. She had written a lot.

I know it's hard to come to a new school and make friends. I'm sorry Susan wasn't sensitive to your feelings. It's what you're like inside that really counts, and that's what your classmates will see once they get to know you. Give Susan another chance to be your friend. Please come and talk

to me when you feel sad or angry. I
understand what you're going through.

Rana shut her journal and put it in her desk.
Her teacher was kind. Rana didn't feel mad at
Susan anymore. She went out to the playground to
see if Susan was there. She wasn't. Rana walked
over to Jenny and Richard.

"How's Tiger?" asked Jenny.

"Not so good," said Rana. "She threw up in my
bedroom."

"Not kitty puke!" Richard made gagging sounds.

"Stop it, Richard," said Jenny. "Can't you see
that Rana's worried?"

"My grandma seemed mad at Tiger," said Rana.
"She wouldn't help me clean up."

"I wouldn't either," said Richard.

Jenny put her hand on Rana's arm. "Cats throw
up a lot. It doesn't mean they're sick."

Rana was horrified. "You mean I might find that
yucky stuff in my room every morning?"

"Not every morning," said Jenny.

"Every other morning," said Richard. He
smiled, showing all his teeth. He looked like a car-
toon cat.

Jenny giggled. Rana found herself giggling, too.

Richard started singing, "Kitty throw-up on the ground, Kitty throw-up all around."

Susan hurried over. "Did you get everything cleaned up?" she asked.

"Yes," said Rana. "Thank you for helping me." She gave Susan a hug.

Later Rana wrote on a new page in her journal:

Kitty throw-up on the ground,
Kitty throw-up all around,
Sometimes I just want to weep,
When kitty does this while I sleep.

She showed the journal entry to Jenny, who laughed and passed it to Richard.

"Write this down," Richard said to Rana. "Kitty throw-up down below, Kitty throw-up on my toe."

Rana laughed and wrote it down.

"If Grandma slips it will be rough," Richard continued the poem. "Vacuum up that yucky stuff."

They all laughed, even Susan.

"What's so funny?" said Mrs. Steele. She leaned over Rana and read her journal.

"Richard wrote most of it," said Rana.

Mrs. Steele laughed. "I didn't know I had so many poets in the class."

Rana smiled. She liked laughing about scary things. Once they were over.

Chapter 10

Rana woke up on Saturday morning to the sound of kitty purring. She opened her eyes. Tiger was sitting on her chest. "There's no school today," she told the cat. "We can both sleep late." Tiger continued to purr. Rana moved the kitty off her chest and rolled over. Tiger climbed on her pillow and played with her hair. Rana got up.

Her grandparents were already at the kitchen table. They had finished eating, but were both reading the paper and drinking tea. Rana fed the kitty, then fixed a bowl of cereal for herself.

As soon as Tiger finished eating, she jumped onto the table. Grandma didn't notice, because she held the newspaper up in front of her face. Tiger rubbed against the back of the paper. "Stop that!" Grandma said sharply. Tiger did it again. Grandma set the paper on the table and Tiger lay down on it. Grandma flicked her hand at the cat. Tiger batted at Grandma's hand with her front paws. Her tail moved up and down. "Stop that!" Grandma said again. She sounded really annoyed.

"She's just trying to play with you," said Rana. She pulled Tiger into her lap.

Tiger stood on Rana's legs and looked into her cereal bowl.

"That cat belongs on the floor," said Grandma, "not on the table."

Rana pushed Tiger's head down. She knew Grandma was mad, but her kitten was curious about everything. At least she'd be home all weekend and could keep Tiger out of trouble. She hoped.

Tara came into the room. "Grandma, I'm going to my friend's party today. I have to get ready."

Grandma smiled at Tara. "I'll help you," she said.

Late that afternoon, Rana read a book. The kitty sat beside her on the couch and slept.

The doorbell rang. When Rana opened the door, Tara burst inside. "Look what I won at the party!" she said. She held up a small bowl with a goldfish inside. "I named him Golden Boy."

"How do you know he's a boy fish?" asked Rana.

"He was bigger than the other fish," said Tara.

"Look, Grandma." Tara stood by the chair where her grandmother was sitting. "Isn't my fish pretty?"

"Yes," said Grandma. "He's a lovely fish. Did you have fun at the birthday party?"

"Yes," said Tara. "Look, I have food for Golden Boy in my party bag." She thrust the bag into Grandma's lap.

Grandma looked inside. "Does he eat candy?" she asked.

"No." Tara giggled. "His food is in the little box." Tara put the bowl on the coffee table. She reached into the bag and pulled out a small box of fish food. "I have to feed him once a day."

"Your daddy had a fish once," said Grandpa.

"He did? Was the fish gold like mine?" asked Tara.

"Yes," said Grandpa.

Tara took some candy out of the bag and stuffed

it into her mouth. "Before you clean the fish's bowl, you have to read this paper," said Tara. She pulled a piece of paper from her pocket.

Grandma looked at the paper. "It says the water has to stand for twenty-four hours before you put the fish in it."

"That's so all the bad stuff can get out of the water," said Tara.

"The chemicals," said Grandma. She held the bag of candy away when Tara reached for another piece. "You'll spoil your appetite. It's almost time for dinner."

Tiger lifted her head and looked around. She stood up slowly, then leaped onto the coffee table and sniffed the bowl.

"No, no!" said Tara, pulling the cat away. "She's going to hurt my fish."

Rana picked up Tiger and sat down on the couch, holding the cat in her lap. But the cat struggled free and jumped onto the coffee table again.

"Oh, no," said Tara.

"I'm watching Tiger," said Rana. "She won't hurt the fish. Look, she can't get her head in the bowl. It's too tiny."

The cat stood with her face over the top of the bowl. The opening *was* too tiny.

"See, the fish is safe," said Rana.

Tiger stuck her paw into the bowl.

"Now she's going to grab my fish," yelled Tara.

"No, bad cat!"

As soon as the cat touched the water, she jerked her paw back out and shook it.

"See," said Rana. "She doesn't like to get her paw wet."

"She'll get the water dirty," said Tara, "if she sticks her paw in it."

"She just washed her paws," said Rana.

Grandma stood up. "Tara, come and help me cook the puris. Rana, you can make the salad."

"What about my fish?" said Tara.

"Golden Boy can set the table," said Rana.

Nobody laughed at Rana's joke.

"Who will guard him?" said Tara, frowning at her sister.

"I'll watch your fish," said Grandpa, looking up from his magazine.

While Grandma rolled the puri dough into round, flat cakes, Rana tore the lettuce into small pieces and dropped them into a bowl. She cut up a tomato and half a cucumber.

Tara took a small rolling pin and flattened a ball of dough.

"Grandma, mine doesn't come out round like yours," said Tara.

"That one looks like a hippopotamus," said Rana.

"It will taste good anyway," said Grandma. She took Tara's dough and dropped it into hot oil.

"Will my dough puff up?" asked Tara.

Grandma tapped the funny looking puri with her spoon. It puffed a little.

"I've finished the salad, Grandma," said Rana.

"Now set the table," Grandma told Rana. "We're almost ready to eat."

When Grandma had cooked the last puri, she called Grandpa for dinner.

Everyone sat at the dining-room table.

"Look at my funny puris, Grandpa," said Tara.

"Very nice," said Grandpa. He picked one up and tasted it.

"Does it taste like a hippo?" asked Tara.

"Yes, it does," said Grandpa, smiling at her. "And I really like hippos."

Rana heard a clunk in the other room. *The room where the cat was alone with the fish.* "I have to check something," she said. She hurried into the family room. The goldfish lay flapping on the rug. Its bowl had fallen off the table. All the water had spilled out. Tiger pushed at the fish with his paw. "Oh, no," Rana said. She pulled the cat away.

Tara ran into the room. "Golden Boy!" she screamed. "That bad cat tried to eat Golden Boy!"

Grandpa rushed into the room, followed by Grandma. He picked up the bowl. "I'll get some water."

"It has to be special water," said Tara.

Rana picked the fish up. It was still breathing. She had to find some water that had been sitting around for a day.

"Is Golden Boy dead?" screamed Tara.

Rana raced to the kitchen. She knelt by the kitty's water bowl. She put the fish in the bowl. It swam around slowly. Good thing she hadn't changed the kitty's water since yesterday.

"Is my fish okay?" screamed Tara.

Rana picked up the bowl. Still kneeling, she held it out to Tara. "The fish is swimming."

"But that's the kitty's bowl," said Tara.

Tiger stood up on her hind legs and tried to look in the bowl.

"No, no, bad cat," said Tara. "Tiger wants to drink my fish."

"That cat is very bad," said Grandma. She cast a sour look at Rana.

"Let's put the bowl in Tara's room," said Grandpa, taking the bowl from Rana.

"Shut the door tight," said Grandma. She grabbed a kitchen towel and mopped up the water that had spilled on the family-room rug.

Rana took the empty fish bowl to the sink, rinsed it, and put new water in it. "In twenty-four hours we can put the fish back in its bowl," she told Grandma. Rana filled another bowl with water for the cat to drink.

"Let's finish eating," said Grandpa, coming back into the kitchen with Tara.

Rana entered the dining room first. Tiger was on the table with her paw in Grandma's lassi, a sweet drink made with yogurt. The cat licked her paw. Rana ran to the table and picked up Tiger, but not before Grandma had seen the cat sitting next to her plate with a paw in her glass.

"That cat has been eating our dinner!" said Grandma.

"Just your drink," said Rana in a low voice.

Grandma looked at her plate. She looked at the tablecloth by her glass. It was wet where the liquid had dripped off the cat's paw. "Throw that bad cat outside! I'm not eating another thing!" Grandma grabbed her plate and her glass and rushed to the sink. She slammed them down.

Grandpa went over to Grandma. He talked to her in their language. His voice was calm.

Grandma was not calm. She shrieked and said something back.

Grandpa said something else.

Rana couldn't understand anything they were saying, but Grandma sounded very angry. Rana held her cat tightly and went to her room. "If you don't stop doing bad things," she told the cat, "Grandma will tell my mother to get rid of you."

The kitty put a soft paw on Rana's face and looked at her with wide, innocent eyes. A tear rolled down Rana's cheek.

"You're my best friend," Rana whispered into the kitty's fur. "I couldn't bear to lose you."

Chapter 11

Tiger, my kitty, has been bad. My mom and dad come home tonight and I'm afraid Grandma will tell them how bad my cat has been. Then my mom will decide to give her away. Tiger jumps on the counter and steals food. She licks the butter. She throws up on the carpet. She even brought a snake into the house. Grandma was really mad. But then the worst thing happened—Tiger almost killed my sister's fish.

Mrs. Steele stopped by Rana's desk and read what she had written. "I'm sorry you're having so much trouble with your kitty," she said.

Susan turned around. "Has Tiger been sick again?"

"No," said Rana, "but she tried to kill my sister's fish."

"Oh, no," said Susan.

"Would you like to read your journal entry to the class?" said Mrs. Steele. "Maybe they can help."

Rana didn't want to read in front of the class. But Mrs. Steele squeezed her shoulder and smiled at her. Rana stood up and read about her naughty kitty.

"You should spray her with water every time she gets on the counter or the table," said Susan. "That way you will teach her to stay off them. I'll come after school to help you. You'll need some kind of spray bottle."

Richard waved his arm in the air.

"Yes, Richard," said Mrs. Steele.

"A water pistol would work," he said.

Everyone laughed.

"You shouldn't let Tiger go outside," said Mary. "Cats kill lots of birds and other animals."

"My neighbor's cat was run over by a car," said Kevin. "I saw it in the street."

"Did it get squashed?" asked Richard.

"No," said Kevin. "It lay on its side like it was asleep."

Rana knew how sad she'd feel if her cat were run over. She decided not to let Tiger go outside anymore.

"Let's think of more ways to help Rana," said Mrs. Steele.

"How did the cat get the fish?" asked Richard.

"She pushed the bowl off the table," said Rana. "It was a little bowl."

"Smart cat," said Kevin. "You should get a bigger bowl. One she couldn't move."

"Does your cat have any toys?" asked Jenny.

"No," said Rana.

"If she had more toys," said Jenny, "she might not play with fish and snakes."

"Okay, class," said Mrs. Steele. "Thanks for giving Rana so many helpful suggestions. Now it's time to get out your math workbooks."

When school was over, Rana and Susan went outside together. "I'll be over soon," Susan promised.

Rana crossed the street and started walking home. She heard Susan call Richard's name. Rana looked back and saw Susan talking with Richard and Jenny. She wished she had as many friends as Susan had. She walked home slowly, kicking at some dry, brown leaves on the sidewalk. She wondered if the kitty had done any more bad things while she was at school. The house was quiet when she entered.

Grandma was in the kitchen. "I made some burfi," she said. "It's an Indian candy. We can have some with tea when Grandpa gets back."

Rana set down her backpack and looked for

Tiger. She found her by the glass door, sleeping in the sun. Tiger lifted her head. Her whiskers looked silver in the light.

Rana picked up the cat and walked back to the kitchen. "Where did Grandpa go?" she asked.

"Grandpa walked Tara to a friend's house," said Grandma. "Tara seems to have made many friends here. She even went to a birthday party."

Rana winced. At least I have my kitty, she thought. She kissed the side of the cat's face. Tiger squirmed and jumped to the floor.

The doorbell rang. It was Susan.

"I brought you a comb to use on Tiger's fur. That way she won't get hair balls." She handed the comb to Rana.

When the two girls entered the kitchen, Grandma's face lit up. "It's nice to see you again, Susan," she said.

"I'm going to tell Rana how to train Tiger," said Susan.

Grandma rolled her eyes. "That cat could certainly use some lessons," she said. "Would you like some cocoa?"

"I would love some," said Susan.

Rana got the cocoa mix from the cupboard.

Grandma put cocoa and milk in a saucepan.

"Sometimes I add a little spice to it," she said. "Would you like to try it that way?"

"Sure," said Susan. She smelled the spices. "What kind of spices are in here?"

"It's my own recipe," said Grandma. "Cardamom, cinnamon, anise, ginger. I put it in Grandpa's tea, too."

Tiger came into the kitchen and Susan picked her up. "Let me show you how to comb her." Susan held Tiger in her lap and combed the kitty's back. "Look at all the fur in this comb." Susan held up the comb. It was full of kitty hair. "If you comb her every day, she won't get so many hair balls."

The doorbell rang. Rana went to answer it.

Richard stood outside with a water pistol in his hand. "I thought you could use this on your cat," he said. "Susan told me I'd better come over, or you might lose your cat."

Rana was so surprised to see Richard that she couldn't think of anything to say. "Uh . . . uh . . . come in," said Rana. "My grandma is making cocoa.

"Grandma, this is Richard," said Rana when they entered the kitchen.

"Hello, Richard," said Grandma. "Are you in

Rana's class too?" She added some more milk and cocoa to the saucepan.

"Yes," said Richard. He spotted Susan and held up the water pistol. "I found it in the bottom of my closet."

"Good. Let's show Rana what to do when Tiger gets on the counter," said Susan. "Richard, is your water pistol full of water?"

"Yep," said Richard.

Susan put Tiger down. The cat sat on the floor looking at them.

"Come on up on the counter, you bad cat," said Richard.

Tiger continued to sit on the floor.

"I know what to do," said Rana. She got a stick of butter out of the refrigerator. She unwrapped the butter, showed it to the cat, then set it on the counter.

Tiger jumped onto the counter and headed for the butter. Richard pulled the trigger. A stream of water hit the cat in the face. Tiger jumped off the counter and ran out of the kitchen.

"See," said Susan. "Cats hate water in their faces."

"Good work, Richard and Susan," said Grandma.

The doorbell rang again. This time it was Jenny. She had brought some toys for the kitty. Tiger was still under one of the dining chairs, hiding out after being sprayed. Jenny held a feather toy in front of the cat. Richard and Susan came out to watch. Tiger reached out a paw to touch the feathers. Jenny pulled the feathers away. Richard tossed some toy mice up in the air. The cat chased them as they scattered across the rug.

Grandma called, "The cocoa is ready."

Everyone went back to the kitchen and sat down.

"This is delicious," said Susan, taking a sip.

"Mmm," said Richard.

"Grandma's spices make it special," said Rana.

Grandma put a bowl on the table. "This is called chevro. It contains cereal and nuts and raisins, but it's spicy. Try a little bit."

Richard tossed a big handful into his mouth. He coughed, drained his cup of cocoa, and said, "That's great stuff." Tears ran down his face.

Grandma poured him some more cocoa. Then she put a plate of orange squares on the table. "If the chevro is too hot, you might like this better."

Richard took a bite. "I love this stuff," he said. "Why is it orange?"

"It's made with carrots," said Grandma. "It's called burfi."

"Can you teach me how to make it?" asked Susan. "It's yummy."

"Of course," said Grandma.

"I want to learn, too," said Jenny.

"I just want to eat it," said Richard.

Tiger jumped onto the table and sniffed Rana's burfi. "No, no, kitty," she said.

"Let me show you how to use this water pistol," said Richard. He handed the pistol to Grandma. "You just aim at the cat and pull the trigger."

Grandma took aim and a stream of water hit the kitty's fur. The cat jumped off the table and tore into the hallway. Grandma chuckled.

"Good shot, Grandma," said Richard.

Grandma smiled at Richard. "Can I keep the water pistol?" she said.

"Sure," said Richard. "It's all yours."

"I'll be sure to use it," said Grandma. She chuckled again.

Rana sat with her mouth open. This wasn't the wrong grandma from the weekend, the one who'd screamed at the cat and thrown her dishes in the sink. Rana hoped that this new grandma would stick around.

Chapter 12

After Susan, Jenny, and Richard went home, Grandma prepared the food for dinner. Rana helped cut up vegetables. Tara helped with the salad. She tore the lettuce into very tiny pieces.

Tiger jumped onto the counter. Grandma pulled the water pistol from her apron pocket and shot water at the cat. Tiger leaped off the counter and raced from the kitchen. With a smile of satisfaction, Grandma put the water pistol back in her pocket. "Richard is a nice boy," said Grandma.

"He makes me laugh," said Rana.

"Yes, I imagine he would," said Grandma.

"Susan's been really nice to me," said Rana.

"Yes, she's a very helpful friend," said Grandma. "And Jenny is very sweet."

"Grandma and I got some books from the library," said Tara. "Can we read one now?"

"Your parents should be home soon," said Grandma. "We can read while we wait for them."

Rana was excited about seeing her parents, but worried at the same time. What would happen when they heard about all the bad things Tiger had done?

Grandma carried a book to the living room. Rana and Tara sat on either side of Grandma on the couch. The story was called *The Tiger Child*. It was an Indian folktale about a tiger cub who was sent to a village by his uncle to get some fire. But the cub kept forgetting what his uncle wanted, and instead drank some fresh milk, ate a delicious fish, lay on a cushion, had his fur combed, and went to sleep by the fire. In the end, the cub forgot his wild ways and became a house cat.

"Our tiger is turning into a cat, too," said Tara when they finished reading the story.

"Were you once a wild tiger?" Rana patted the kitty sleeping beside her.

The kitten raised her head.

"She's still a bit wild," said Grandma. Tiger stood up and walked across Rana's lap to Grandma. She stood on Grandma's lap with her tail in

Grandma's face. "What does the cat want?" said Grandma, pushing the cat's tail to one side. The cat turned around and sat down.

"She wants to be your friend," said Rana.

The cat heard the car in the driveway before anyone else did. She lifted her head and her ears swiveled toward the front door.

"What is it?" said Rana.

The cat hopped to the floor. Then Rana heard footsteps on the porch and the door opened.

"Hi, we're home," said Dad.

Mom came into the living room first. Tara rushed into her arms. "We missed you," said Mom, giving Tara a hug. She looked over at Rana and Grandma. "How did everything go while we were gone?"

"Fine, fine," said Grandpa.

"No problems?" said Dad. He looked first at Grandpa and then at Grandma.

"No, not really," said Grandma.

The cat rubbed Mom's ankles. "And the cat was okay?"

Rana looked at Grandma and held her breath. Grandma looked thoughtful. She opened her mouth to say something, but Tara started talking.

"The kitty almost ate my new fish," said Tara.

Uh-oh. Here comes a bad cat tale, Rana thought.

"You have a new fish?" said Mom, raising her eyebrows.

"Yes, and his bowl fell off the table," said Tara.

"Oh, dear," said Mom.

"But Rana saved Golden Boy," said Tara. "She put him in Tiger's water bowl."

"Really?" said Dad, sitting down.

The kitty climbed into Dad's lap.

"Rana forgot to change the kitty's water," said Tara, "but that was good, because the fish needs old water."

"Old water?" said Dad.

"Yes, you can't use water from the sink," said Tara. "It has bad stuff in it."

"Oh, right," said Dad. He looked at Mom. She still had her coat on.

"Anything else happen?" asked Mom.

"Tell them about the snake, Grandma," said Tara.

"The snake?" said Mom. She sat down in the rocking chair.

"The kitty caught a snake," said Grandpa. "But I took it outside."

"The snake was inside?" said Dad.

"Tiger brought it to me," said Rana. "I think it was a present."

Mom rolled her eyes. "I'm sorry the cat was such a problem," she said. "I knew I shouldn't have let Rana keep that cat."

Rana went over to Dad. She took the cat from his lap and hugged her tight. "I love my cat," she said. Tears filled her eyes.

"Now just a minute," said Grandma.

Rana held her breath.

"True, the cat needs some training," Grandma began, "but it's a very friendly animal." She looked at Rana. "The cat helped Rana make friends at school," Grandma continued. "Rana looks happier than I've ever seen her. I think you really must keep Tiger."

Mom stared at Grandma.

Rana stared at Grandma.

"Oh," said Mom.

Rana ran over to Grandma and gave her a kiss.

"But before I leave, I'll have to give you something," Grandma told Mom. She reached into the pocket of her apron and pulled out the water pistol. "This keeps the cat off the table."

The cat jumped out of Rana's arms and hid under a chair.

"Grandma's a good shot," said Rana.

Everyone laughed.

The next day, Rana got to school early. She opened her desk and pulled out her journal. She had important things to write.

Last night Mom and Dad came home. I was so scared Grandma would say that Tiger had been bad. But my new friends came after school to help me. Susan showed Grandma and me how to train my cat. Richard brought a water pistol. And Jenny brought some cat toys.

Jenny stood by Rana's desk. "How was Tiger after we left?"

Rana looked up from her writing. "Tiger was good. Grandma used the water pistol on her."

"And it worked?" asked Jenny.

"The cat runs away whenever Grandma pulls the water pistol out," said Rana.

Jenny giggled.

Richard walked into the room just as the second bell rang. After he hung up his coat, he stood at the pencil sharpener, sharpening one pencil after another.

"You must be getting ready to write a lot," said Mrs. Steele.

"I'm going to write about what happened after school yesterday," said Richard. "I taught Rana's grandma to shoot a water pistol."

"You did?" said Mrs. Steele.

"Yes," said Richard. "And she gave us some orange stuff to eat."

"Orange stuff?" Mrs. Steele looked at Rana.

"It's called burfi," said Rana, smiling.

"Barfie?" said Kevin. "As in cat barfie?"

"No," said Richard. "Burfi. It's like candy. People eat it in India."

After Richard sat down, Susan turned around and whispered to Rana. "Did your parents come home?"

"Yes," said Rana.

"And what did they say?" asked Susan. "Can you keep your kitty?"

"Yes," said Rana. "I can keep Tiger. Thanks to my grandma."

"Really?" said Susan. "She's not mad at Tiger anymore?"

"Grandma told my parents that I need Tiger," said Rana.

"I'm going to write about your grandma again," said Susan, "but I promise not to read it to the class."

Rana smiled at her friend. "I don't mind," she said. "You can read it out loud to everyone."